THE
LIBRARY FISH

*For my mother, who filled our weekly trips to
the library with a lifelong love of reading!*
—A. S. C.

*For my mom—thank you for all of
the visits to the library when I was little*
—G. J.

SIMON & SCHUSTER BOOKS FOR YOUNG READERS •
An imprint of Simon & Schuster
Children's Publishing Division • 1230 Avenue of
the Americas, New York, New York 10020 • Text © 2022
by Alyssa Satin Capucilli • Illustration © 2022 by Gladys Jose • Book
design by Laurent Linn © 2022 by Simon & Schuster, Inc. • All rights reserved,
including the right of reproduction in whole or in part in any form. • SIMON
& SCHUSTER BOOKS FOR YOUNG READERS and related marks are trademarks of
Simon & Schuster, Inc. • For information about special discounts for bulk purchases, please
contact Simon & Schuster Special Sales at 1-866-506-1949 or business@simonandschuster
.com. • The Simon & Schuster Speakers Bureau can bring authors to your live event. For more
information or to book an event, contact the Simon & Schuster Speakers Bureau at 1-866-248-3049
or visit our website at www.simonspeakers.com. • The text for this book was set in Banda Regular. •
The illustrations for this book were rendered digitally with original textures and collage elements using
Photoshop. • Manufactured in China • 1221 SCP • First Edition • 10 9 8 7 6 5 4 3 2 1 • Library of
Congress Cataloging-in-Publication Data • Names: Capucilli, Alyssa Satin, 1957– author. | Jose, Gladys,
illustrator. • Title: The Library Fish / Alyssa Satin Capucilli ; illustrated by Gladys Jose. • Description:
First edition. | New York : Simon & Schuster Books for Young Readers, [2022] | "A Paula Wiseman
Book." | Audience: Ages 4-8. | Audience: Grades 2-3. | Summary: When snow prevents Mr. Hughes
from opening the library one day, book-loving Library Fish finds a way to entertain herself and
her bookmobile friend, • Identifiers: LCCN 2020053249 (print) | LCCN 2020053250 (ebook) |
ISBN 9781534477056 (hardcover) | ISBN 9781534477063 (ebook) • Subjects: CYAC: Fishes—
Fiction. | Libraries—Fiction. | Books and reading—Fiction. | Bookmobiles—Fiction. •
Classification: LCC PZ7.C179 Lf 2022 (print) | LCC PZ7.C179 (ebook) | DDC [E]—
dc23 • LC record available at https://lccn.loc.gov/2020053249 • LC ebook
record available at https://lccn.loc.gov/2020053250

THE
LIBRARY FISH

Written by
Alyssa Satin Capucilli

Illustrated by
Gladys Jose

A PAULA WISEMAN BOOK
SIMON & SCHUSTER BOOKS FOR YOUNG READERS
NEW YORK LONDON TORONTO SYDNEY NEW DELHI

Once there was a fish. She was not an ordinary fish. She didn't live in the sea or the ocean. She didn't live in a river or lake. In fact, when Mr. Hughes the librarian found her, he said, "I'm not quite sure where you came from, but, if you love stories, you've come to the right place. Some libraries have their lions, but this library will have you, Fish."

Hard as it might be to believe, Mr. Hughes was sure the fish wiggled her tail. She may have even smiled. From that day on, she was known as Library Fish. She made her home on the desk of Mr. Hughes. It was the perfect place to welcome all the visitors to the library. From where she sat, Library Fish could check each book that was borrowed and returned.

Library Fish quickly grew to love Story Time. Mr. Hughes read stories that made her laugh out loud. He read poems that filled her with wonder. Mr. Hughes read in a bold voice. He read in a whisper.

Library Fish met characters
who were brave and kind,
while others were daring, shy,
or inventive.

Library Fish learned
about distant planets
she might visit
one day.

Of course, Library Fish enjoyed an outing, too. She loved days spent on the bookmobile. Winding through busy streets, Library Fish could feel the excitement of the crowd awaiting their arrival.

I need a long book for the road.

Poetry, please?

I want an adventure!

Any books about puppies?

What's the latest in the Wizzy Wizard series?

Mr. Hughes made sure everyone found just the right book. He always chose something wonderful to read aloud, too. Hard as it might be to believe, Library Fish was certain the bookmobile enjoyed a good story as much as she did. She could feel his engine rumble with joy!

One morning, Library Fish awoke bright and early. She waited for Mr. Hughes to arrive with his usual *Good morning, Library Fish*. She waited and waited, but the library doors remained closed. Where could Mr. Hughes be?

Library Fish looked out over the shelves. Every book sat patiently in its place.

She looked out of the long windows. Could it be?

There, for as far as she could see, was snow—thick snow, falling faster and harder than Library Fish had ever seen before! It reminded her of a story Mr. Hughes read, where snow fell so high and wide, it made busy city streets come to a stop. Could snow make the library come to a stop, too?

Library Fish swam around her bowl. She hummed a tune. She did some fancy spins. The snow kept falling; the library grew quieter and quieter. There was only one thing to do.

"The library may be closed on the outside," said Library Fish, "but it's always open on the inside. There's a story waiting for me; I just have to find it."

Library Fish jumped.

She leaped.

She wiggled.

She didn't get far at all.
"**Hmpfh!**" she said.

Library Fish remembered
the story of a magic beanstalk.
She reached and stretched.

She climbed to the
tip-top of her bowl,
until . . . she slid down
with a **PLOP!**

"Aargh!" she sighed.

"Maybe I can fly up, up, and away like a superhero," said Library Fish. The thing was, she didn't have a cape.

Library Fish looked out of her bowl. The moon peeked through the snowfall.

"That's it!" said Library Fish. "If a rocket ship can soar to the moon, maybe I can . . ."

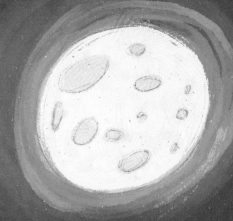

"Five-four-three-two-one . . . **blast of**

she shouted.

And with one big splash, Library Fish landed safely at the foot of a towering stack of books! Filled with all the possibility of a great story, she set off at once. Library Fish looked over the book cart.

Some of the books were too ^{high} to reach.

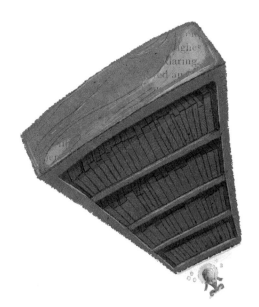

Some were too **heavy**.

Library Fish went up and down the aisles. She passed shelf after shelf until she found just what she was looking for.

There, in the Story Time corner, were plenty of books, ready for reading! Library Fish settled into a comfortable, cozy spot. She opened cover after cover. She turned page after page. She pored over wonderful illustrations. And before long something extraordinary happened. . . .

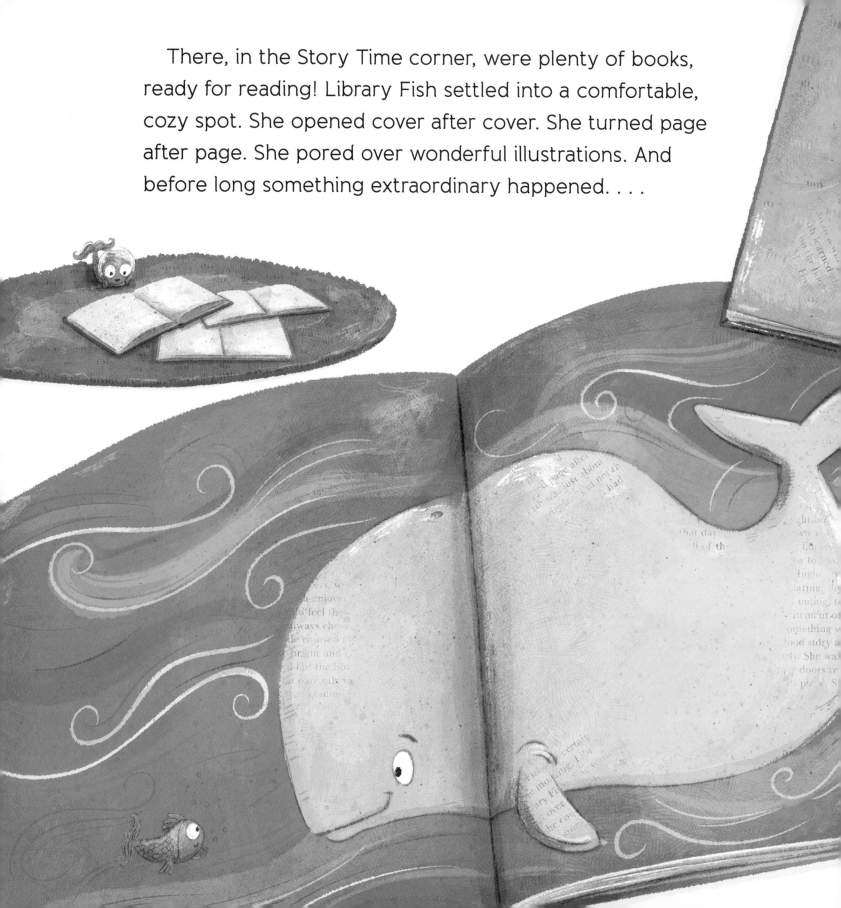

Library Fish was just about to reach for one more story when she heard it. First, a BEEP! Then, a HONK! And then, *VROOM, VROOM!*
"Why didn't I think of this sooner?" Library Fish said with a giggle.
"I'm not the only one around here who loves a good story."

Library Fish chose some of her very favorite books. And although it had already been a night filled with adventures, she was sure there was time for just a few more.

Library Fish read in a **bold** voice. She read in a whisper.

She read until she laughed out loud. She read until she felt the bookmobile's engine rumble with joy. And before long something extraordinary happened again!

When the first rays of sun began to shine, a very tired Library Fish climbed back into her bowl. She dreamed wonderful dreams, until . . .

"Good morning, Library Fish," said Mr. Hughes. "Are you ready to welcome our visitors?"

She was ready, indeed. Library Fish smiled. She wiggled her tail.

Hard as it might be to believe, Mr. Hughes was sure Library Fish yawned, too.